For Joe and Jenny

Copyright © 1997 by Julie Scott.
The rights of Julie Scott to be identified as the author and illustrator of this
work have been asserted by her in accordance with the Copyright, Designs
and Patents Act, 1988.
First published in Great Britain in 1997 by Andersen Press Ltd., 20 Vauxhall
Bridge Road, London SW1V 2SA. Published in Australia by Random House
Australia Pty., 20 Alfred Street, Milsons Point, Sydney, NSW 2061. All rights
reserved. Colour separated in England by In-House Colour Ltd., London.
Printed and bound in Italy by Grafiche AZ, Verona.

10   9   8   7   6   5   4   3   2   1

British Library Cataloguing in Publication Data available.
ISBN 0 86264 704 5

This book has been printed on acid-free paper

Sleepy Kitten

Julie Scott

Andersen Press • London

"I want to sleep," yawned Daisy.
But the other kittens wanted to play.

"The mat looks like the perfect place," decided Daisy.
But it wasn't.

Daisy ran upstairs
as fast as she could.

She peeped in the playroom. "I can see a cosy corner in here," she thought.

But it wasn't.

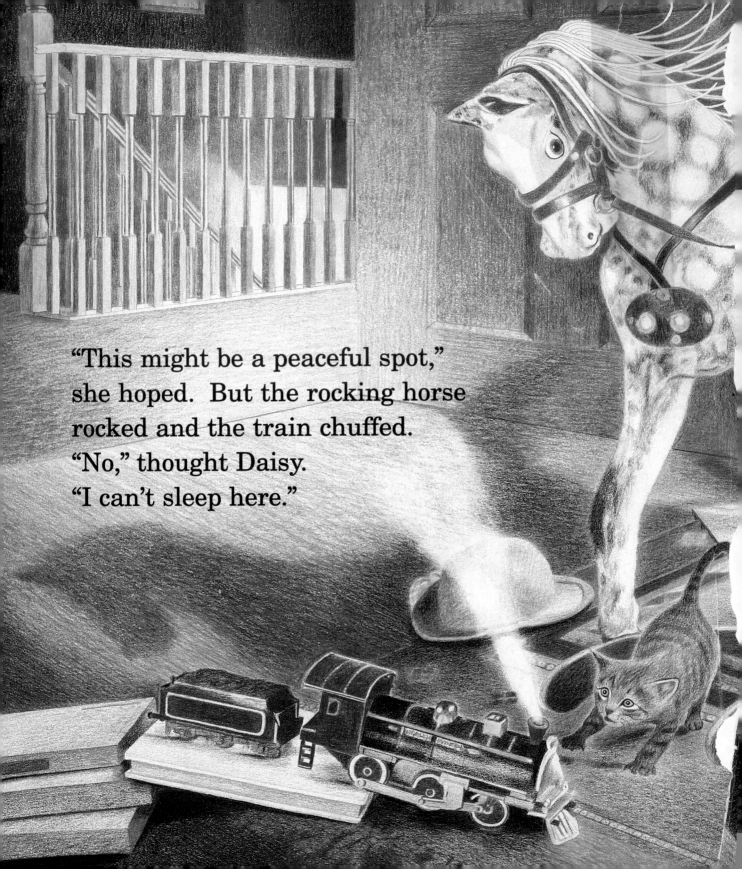

"This might be a peaceful spot,"
she hoped. But the rocking horse
rocked and the train chuffed.
"No," thought Daisy.
"I can't sleep here."

The jack-in-a-box jumped up.
Daisy jumped down.

The soldiers went "charge!"
Daisy went dizzy.

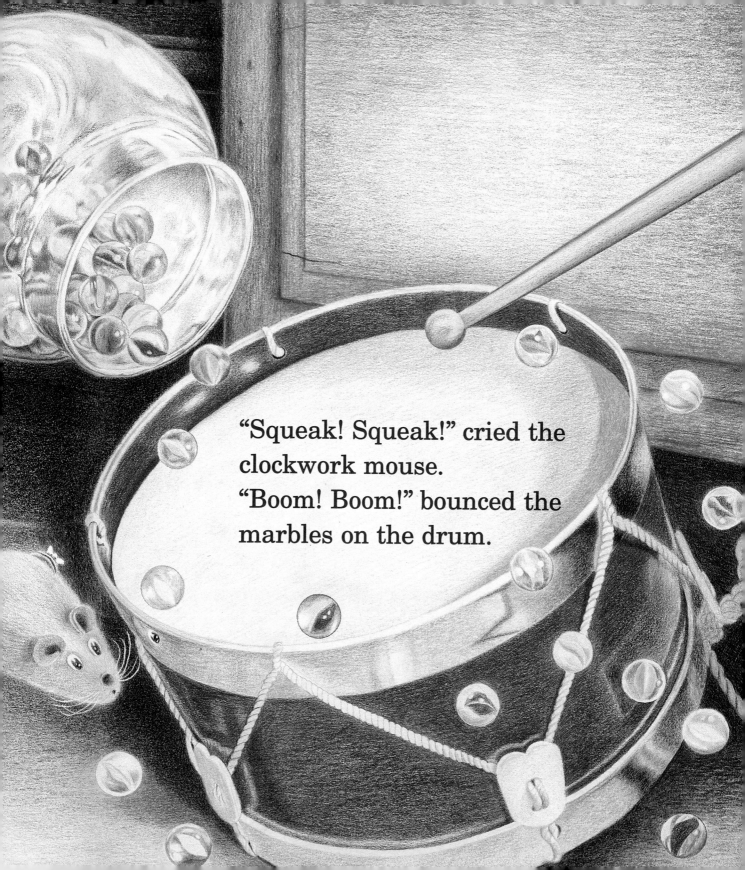

"Squeak! Squeak!" cried the
clockwork mouse.
"Boom! Boom!" bounced the
marbles on the drum.

"Crash!" went the castle bricks.
"Mama!" cried the doll.
"Help!" cried Daisy. "I can't sleep here."
Daisy jumped as high as she could.

"Oh, where can I sleep?" sighed Daisy.
Suddenly, everything was quiet and still.
Daisy's ears twitched. Could this be the place?

And it was. Nothing moved
and nothing squeaked...
But as Daisy smiled and
snuggled up, Tartan Ted
winked. Then he whispered
softly, "Sweet dreams,"
and switched off the lamp.